The Missing Bag

By Elsie Nelley
Illustrations by Nathalie Ortega

Contents

Chapter 1

At the Airport

On Friday, I went to the airport with Mum and Dad. Sofu and Sobo were coming to stay with us for a holiday.

They live far away in Japan.

Dad and I went upstairs.
We saw the big plane from Japan land on the runway.

Dad and I went back downstairs,
and we sat beside Mum.
We waited for Sofu and Sobo
to come out with their bags.

Lots of people from Japan came out with their bags.

But we did not see Sofu and Sobo.

We waited for a long time!

Chapter 2

Sobo's Bag

At last, we saw Sofu and Sobo.
Sofu was pulling his big bag
behind him.
He had his other arm around Sobo.
She looked upset.

Sobo told us that her big bag
was missing.
It had been on the plane
when they left Japan.
Now, it was lost!

The people who worked at the airport said they would find Sobo's bag. They would bring it to our house.

It was dark outside
when we left the airport.

Mum and Dad walked beside Sobo
on the way to our car.
I walked beside Sofu.

I was hungry.
Sofu was hungry, too.

Mum said we could have dinner on the way home.

Chapter 3

Dinner with Sofu and Sobo

Mum and Dad took us to a **restaurant**. There were lots of people inside the restaurant.

We could hear them talking. We could see them eating with **chopsticks**. We could see big pictures of places in Japan on the walls.

Sofu liked the restaurant.
But Sobo was still upset.

I sat down with Mum and Dad
at a long table.
Sofu and Sobo sat down, too.
On the other side of the table
was a **hotplate**.

A woman came and cooked our dinner
on the hotplate.
I watched her.
She was very clever.

The woman talked to Sofu and made him laugh. Mum and Dad laughed, too.

We had little bowls of rice
to eat with our dinner.

Sofu was the best
at holding chopsticks.

Then, Sobo's phone rang.

She told us that someone at the airport
had found her bag.
A man would bring it to our place
in the morning.

Sobo clapped her hands.
At last, she began to smile.
Her bag had been found!

Glossary

chopsticks sticks for eating food

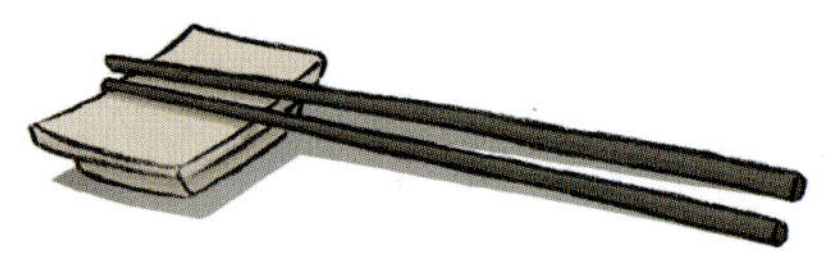

hotplate a plate for cooking food

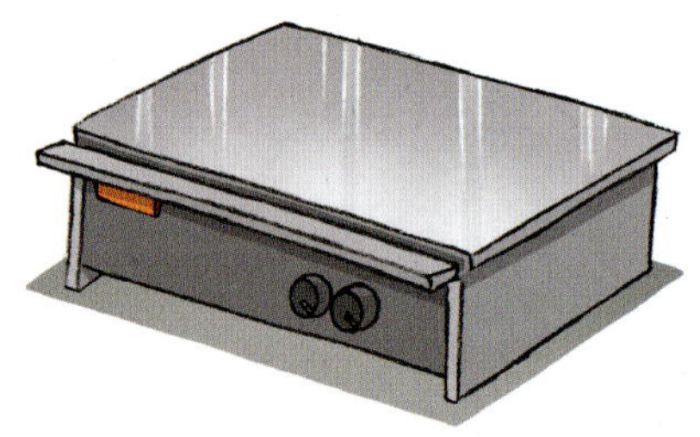

restaurant a place to eat food

The Missing Bag

Text: Elsie Nelley
Series consultant: Annette Smith
Publishing editor: Simone Calderwood
Editor: Rachel Day
Project editor: Eliza Webb
Designer: Kerri Wilson
Series designer: Karen Mayo
Illustrations: Nathalie Ortega
Production controller: Erin Dowling
Reprint: Siew Han Ong

PM Guided Reading

Orange Level 16

Nippers Beach Fun
How to Make a Racing Car
The Troll Under the Bridge
Animals that Live Under the Ground
The Missing Bag
The Peacock and the Crane
Our Beach Camping Ground
The Ribbon Dance
Windy Days
Sleeping at School!

ISBN 978 0 17 026628 4

Cengage Learning Australia
Level 5 , 80 Dorcas Street
Southbank VIC 3006
Phone: 1300 790 853
Email: aust.nelsonprimary@cengage.com

For learning solutions, visit cengage.com.au

Printed in China by 1010 Printing International Ltd
15 24

15

PM Level 16

17

18

19

20

21

22

23

24

25

26

27

28

29

30

I was so happy! Sofu and Sobo, my grandparents, were coming all the way from Japan to stay with us. But when we met them at the airport, Sobo looked upset! What could be the matter with her?

Text Type:
Recount (Imaginative)

Sparrow's Lesson

Retold by Jill McDougall

Illustrations by Valerie Valdivia

Sparrow's Lesson

Level 19

Running Words 464 **Text Type** Narrative (Fable)

Curriculum Areas English (Literacy, Literature, Language); Humanities (Civics and Citizenship)

Retelling to Encourage Critical Thinking About the Content

Ask each student to retell the story in their own words.

Record the retelling for further discussion and reflection.

Questions to Reinforce Meaning and Stimulate Discussion

Literal

1 Why was Sparrow cross with Crow?

2 What did Sparrow ask Flea to do?

3 What was the small thing Crow found and put underneath his wing?

Inferential

4 Why did Sparrow want Mouse to chew Old Pony's tail?

5 Why did Sparrow think Cat would be able to frighten Mouse?

6 Why didn't the other animals do what Sparrow asked them to do?

7 How did Sparrow upset everyone?

8 What was Sparrow's lesson?

Applied Knowledge

9 What is another animal that could have been in this story? Why?

10 How did Crow show he is a good friend to Sparrow?

Links with Other PM Guided Reading Books

Level 19	Narrative	*A Dog Called Bear*
Level 19	Narrative	*The Pedlar's Caps*
Level 19	Narrative (Play)	*The Best Animal in the Forest*
Level 20	Narrative	*Penny and the Falcons*
Level 20	Narrative	*Dinner Time for Ruff*